The Magic Key

Red Planet

Story by Roderick Hunt

Illustrations by Alex Brychta

D0995734

OXFORD
UNIVERSITY PRESS

Titles in the series

Wilf came to play with Chip.

They made a rocket ship out of bits and pieces.

The rocket ship looked quite good.

Wilf and Chip played in the rocket ship.

They pretended to be spacemen.

'The rocket is going to take off,' said Wilf.

'Five ... four ... three ... two ...'

Floppy ran up.

He wanted to get in the rocket ship with
Wilf and Chip.

'Go away, Floppy,' called Chip.

'The rocket is going to take off!'

Nadim came to play.

He had his computer with him, but he

liked the look of the rocket ship.

He wanted to play on it too.

Just then, it began to rain.

'There's not room for all of us,' said Chip.

'Let's go inside and play with Nadim's computer.'

They played a game on the computer.

It was called Red Planet.

They had to land a rocket on the planet.

Wilf and Chip crashed the rocket.

Nadim didn't. He was good at the game.

Suddenly, the magic key began to glow.

Chip and Wilf pulled Nadim away from the

computer and ran into Biff's room.

'Come on,' called Chip. 'It's time for

an adventure.'

The magic took them to a rocket ship.

It took Floppy too.

The rocket looked as if it was about to take off, but the door was open.

Nadim wanted to look inside the rocket.

'Come on,' he called.

Chip didn't want to go inside. 'It may not be safe,' he said.

'Why not?' said Nadim. 'This is a magic key adventure.'

They went inside the rocket.

There was nobody there.

'Look at this computer,' said Nadim.

Floppy jumped up and put his paw on a button.

Five … four … three … two … one.

The rocket began to take off.

Up it went and out into space.

'Oh no!' said Chip. 'I don't know where
we're going.'

They began to float about inside the rocket.

Nadim found some boots.

He put them on.

'We must put these boots on,' he said.

'They will keep us down on the floor.'

They went to the window and looked out.

They saw a big red planet.

'We are going to land on that planet,' said Nadim.

'We will soon be there.'

Nadim made the rocket land.

'I wouldn't like to do that again,' he said.

'It's a good job Nadim knows about computers,' thought Wilf.

'I wouldn't like to crash here.'

There was red dust all over the planet.

There were red rocks and red mountains.

Floppy didn't like the look of it.

He began to bark and bark.

'There are no trees,' he thought.

They wanted to go outside and look at
the planet.
They found a space buggy.
They looked in the space buggy and
found some spacesuits.

'Let's put these spacesuits on,' said Wilf.

'Then we can go outside.'

'Do you think it will be safe outside?'
asked Chip.

'I don't know,' said Wilf.

They went out on the planet in the buggy.
The buggy bumped over the rocks and the
red dust flew up.
'I don't like this,' thought Floppy. 'I'm not
made for space adventures.'

Suddenly the ground cracked and a big
hole opened up.

'Oh help,' said Chip, Wilf, and Nadim as
the buggy fell into the hole.

They fell down and down inside the planet.

'I don't like this,' thought Floppy. 'I want
to go home.'

They all landed with a bump.

The buggy landed with a crash and broke in two.

They were inside a big cave.

'What a place!' said Wilf. 'Look at it.'

Chip looked at the buggy.

'It's broken,' he said. 'It's had it!

How will we get back to the rocket?'

Floppy began to bark.

There were some creatures in the cave.

They looked like funny little people.

'Oh no!' said Nadim. 'Look at them!

I hope they like us.'

The creatures looked at the boys.

They climbed on the broken buggy and

pulled out a spacesuit.

One of them turned a tap on

Floppy's spacesuit.

Floppy's spacesuit began to fill with air.

It got bigger and bigger.

Then Floppy began to float.

'Get Floppy!' yelled Chip. 'Don't let
him float away!'

Wilf asked the creatures how to get out of
the cave.

They told him that there was no way out.

They said that they had never been outside.

Wilf had a good idea.

He took a spacesuit out and he filled it with air.

The spacesuit got bigger and bigger.

It began to float up and up.

'Hold on,' called Wilf, 'and don't let go!'

The spacesuit floated up out of the cave.

'We can float back to the rocket,' said

Chip. 'What a good idea!'

'I hope it won't go pop,' thought Floppy.

They floated back to the rocket.

Wilf let the air out of the spacesuit and it
came down to the ground.

'Good old Wilf!' said Nadim.

'I don't like floating,' thought Floppy.

They went inside the rocket and it took off.

Nadim turned on the computer and

looked at the screen.

'We'll soon be home,' he said.

Just then the magic key began to glow.

'That's good,' thought Floppy. 'They won't
have to land the rocket.

Dogs don't like space adventures.'

The magic took them back home.

'I liked that adventure,' said Wilf.

He looked at the little spacesuit.

'So did I,' said Nadim, 'but I'm glad I didn't have to land that rocket again.'

Questions about the story

- What two games did the children play before the adventure?
- Who went on this Magic Key adventure?
- Who made the rocket take off?
- Who landed the rocket?
- Who didn't enjoy the adventure?
- What did they all have to wear on the planet?
- Where did the yellow creatures live?
- How did Floppy's suit get blown up?
- How did Chip save him from floating away?
- What did they bring back from this adventure?

OXFORD
UNIVERSITY PRESS

Great Clarendon Street, Oxford OX2 6DP

Oxford University Press is a department of the University of Oxford.
It furthers the University's objective of excellence in research, scholarship,
and education by publishing worldwide in

Oxford New York

Athens Auckland Bangkok Bogotá Buenos Aires Calcutta Cape Town
Chennai Dar es Salaam Delhi Florence Hong Kong Istanbul Karachi
Kuala Lumpur Madrid Melbourne Mexico City Mumbai Nairobi
Paris São Paulo Shanghai Singapore Taipei Tokyo Toronto Warsaw

with associated companies in Berlin Ibadan

Oxford is a registered trade mark of Oxford University Press
in the UK and in certain other countries

British Library Cataloguing in Publication Data

Data available

ISBN 0 19 919426 2

Printed in Hong Kong